Whale, Quail, Snail

When Whales Fly

by Erica S. Perl
illustrated by Sam Ailey

Ready-to-Read

Simon Spotlight
New York London Toronto Sydney New Delhi

To Phin and Sarah, who know the difference between real friends and rock friends (and are excellent collectors of both)
— E. S. P.

For Pauline and Paul, thank you for everything — S. A.

SIMON SPOTLIGHT
An imprint of Simon & Schuster Children's Publishing Division
1230 Avenue of the Americas, New York, New York 10020
This Simon Spotlight edition May 2022

For information about special discounts for bulk purchases, please contact Simon & Schuster Special Sales at 1-866-506-1949 or business@simonandschuster.com.
Manufactured in the United States of America 0322 LAK
2 4 6 8 10 9 7 5 3 1
Library of Congress Cataloging-in-Publication Data
Names: Perl, Erica S., author. | Ailey, Sam, illustrator.
Title: When whales fly / by Erica S. Perl ; illustrated by Sam Ailey.
Description: Simon Spotlight edition. | New York : Simon Spotlight, 2022.
Series: Whale, quail, snail | Summary: Whale wants to fly, and Snail offers to teach her, but Quail insists that whales cannot fly.
Identifiers: LCCN 2021041080 | ISBN 9781534497320 (paperback) | ISBN 9781534497337 (hardcover) | ISBN 9781534497344 (ebook)
Subjects: LCSH: Whales—Juvenile fiction. | Snails—Juvenile fiction. | Quails—Juvenile fiction. | Friendship—Juvenile fiction. | CYAC: Whales—Fiction. | Snails—Fiction. | Quails—Fiction. | Friendship—Fiction. | LCGFT: Picture books.
Classification: LCC PZ7.P3163 Whe 2022 | DDC [E]—dc23
LC record available at https://lccn.loc.gov/2021041080

It was a sunny day on Tiny Island.
Whale was watching the clouds
with her friends, Quail and Snail.

"Wow!" Whale sighed.
"I wish I could fly."
"You can," said Snail.

"I can?" asked Whale.

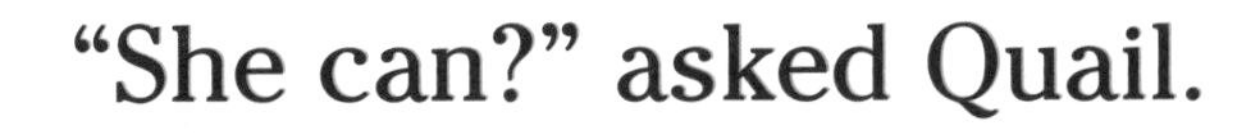

"She can?" asked Quail.

"Sure," said Snail.
"We will teach her."

“We will?” asked Quail.
“We will!” said Snail.
Snail took a rope.
They tied one end to
their surfboard
and the other to Whale.

Then Whale, Quail, and Snail swam and paddled out.

"Is it flying time?" asked Whale.
"Not yet," said Snail. "First, you have to think very light thoughts."
"Very light thoughts," repeated Whale. She closed her eyes.

"Snail," whispered Quail.
"This is not going to work.
Whale is a whale.
And whales can't fly."

But Snail didn't hear Quail.
Snail was too busy watching Whale.
Whale was trying to think
very light thoughts.

Let's see . . . clouds are light,
thought Whale.
Cotton candy is light. Very light!
Whale bobbed happily.
Then she opened her eyes.
"Is it working?" she asked.

"Not yet," said Snail.
"Now you have to sing a flying song."
"Snail?!" said Quail, a little louder.
"This is not going to work.
Whale is a whale.
And whales can't fly."

But Snail didn't hear Quail.
Snail was too busy listening to
Whale sing.
"I will fly, way up high,
in the sky, pizza pie!" Whale sang,
and then asked, "Is it working now?"

“Getting there,” said Snail.
“Next, you have to take
a deep breath and . . .”

"SNAIL!" yelled Quail.
"This is NOT going to work.
Whale is a whale.
And WHALES CAN'T FLY!"

For a moment,
it was very quiet and still.

Then Snail's surfboard
started to rock from side to side.

And Whale began to wail.

HOO

"Oh, Whale! I am so sorry," said Quail.
"It's no big deal that you can't fly.
You're a great swimmer.
And you're a wonderful friend!"

Whale shook her head.
She was too upset to say anything.
She started to swim away.

“Whale! Wait! Hang on!” called Snail.

But Whale didn't hear Snail.
Whale was too busy swimming faster.

And faster.

And then . . .

"Way to go, Whale!" cheered Snail.
"See, Quail?" said Snail.
"I told you we could teach Whale to fly."
Snail looked around for Quail.

"Help!" cried Quail. "I can't swim!"

Luckily, Whale could swim.

"We can teach you," she told Quail.
"We can?!" asked Snail.

"Sure," said Whale. "I'm a great swimmer."

Quail nodded. "You're pretty good at flying, too."

“Thanks!” said Whale, smiling proudly.
“And don’t worry,” she added.
“Swimming is just as easy as flying.”

THE END